THE PUPPY

GIZMO

THE PUPPY PLACE

**Don't miss any of these
other stories by Ellen Miles!**

THE PUPPY PLACE

GIZMO

ELLEN MILES

SCHOLASTIC INC.

For the real Carmen, with thanks
from me and Zipper

No part of this publication may be reproduced, stored in a retrieval
system, or transmitted in any form or by any means, electronic,
mechanical, photocopying, recording, or otherwise, without written
permission of the publisher. For information regarding permission,
write to Scholastic Inc., Attention: Permissions Department,
557 Broadway, New York, NY 10012.

ISBN 978-0-545-60380-5

Cover art by Tim O'Brien
Original cover design by Steve Scott

12 11 10 9 8 7 6 5 4 3 2   13 14 15 16 17 18/0

Printed in the U.S.A.   40

First printing, October 2013

CHAPTER ONE

"Dr. Lopez will be with you and Charles soon, Mrs. Peterson. You can take a seat over there." Martha, the receptionist, pointed to some comfy-looking chairs next to a big fish tank.

"Thanks," said Charles's mom.

"Great," mumbled Charles. He did not want to see Dr. Lopez soon. He did not want to see her at all. It wasn't that she was mean. She was probably the nicest doctor in the world. She usually asked Charles for his latest knock-knock joke and let him listen to his own heart through her stethoscope. He loved the collection of Matchbox cars she kept in her office, and he didn't mind at all when she stuck that thingy into his ears to have a look around. But there was one thing he did mind.

Shots.

Charles had learned to look away so he couldn't see the size of the needle she was about to stick into his arm. He knew to take deep breaths so he wouldn't feel as nervous. He even remembered that shots never actually hurt that much. He still did not like them. He did not like the smell of the alcohol Dr. Lopez used to clean his arm, he did not like the moment right before she put the needle in, and he did not like the way his arm sometimes felt sore afterward.

"Why do I have to get a shot and Lizzie and the Bean don't?" Charles asked. "It's not fair."

"They'll get flu shots, too," said Mom. "I just wanted to get you in here first because you also need Dr. Lopez to sign off before you start basketball, remember?"

Remember? How could he forget? Charles shut his eyes. Basketball. Everybody was excited about the new after-school program that Coach Ridley was starting. Charles's best friends, Sammy and David, had signed up, and it was all they were talking about. They couldn't wait to get started. Charles had signed up, too. He pretended to be as excited as everybody else. But secretly, he was dreading the first day of practice. With luck, maybe Dr. Lopez would find something wrong with him. Just a little bit wrong. Just wrong enough that he would have an excuse.

"Why do we have to get shots, anyway, when we're not even sick?" Charles grumbled, as he watched a shiny blue fish chase a tiny yellow one around the fish tank.

"It's to keep you from getting sick," Mom reminded him. "Just like when we bring Buddy to Dr. Gibson for his shots."

Buddy was the Petersons' brown-and-white puppy, and Dr. Gibson was his vet. Charles knew Dr. Gibson well, since the Petersons brought all their foster puppies to see her. The Petersons — Charles and his parents and his older sister, Lizzie, and his younger brother, the Bean — took care of puppies who needed homes. They kept each one until they found it the perfect forever family. Buddy was the only foster puppy who had come to stay for good. Maybe that was because Buddy just happened to be the best puppy ever.

Dr. Gibson was just as nice as Dr. Lopez, but Buddy did not love going to the vet. "Most of the puppies I've known hate getting shots, too," Charles said to his mother, "even though Dr. Gibson gives them dog cookies when they're in her exam room." He wondered about that. Maybe Dr. Lopez should hand out people cookies. Would munching on a chocolate-chip cookie make him feel any better about getting shots?

The outside door banged open and Charles heard kids laughing and shouting. Two stocky toddlers in overalls, about the Bean's age, ran into the waiting room. They looked exactly alike, with brown curls and big brown eyes. They pushed and shoved each other, heading straight for the fish tank. "Don't touch it!" called a voice. A woman with a very, very big belly lumbered after them, sighing as she watched them put their hands — and noses — up against the tank. "Tony, Marco, what did I just tell you?"

At the desk, Martha just shrugged. "It's okay, Mrs. Cavallo," she said. "Kids do that all the time."

The woman sighed again and reached for a chair. Holding her belly with one hand, she sank into it. "Come on, boys." She patted the seat next to her. "Sit here with me."

"Twins?" Charles's mom smiled at the woman.

Mrs. Cavallo nodded. She pointed to her stomach. "And triplets on the way — any day now."

Mom gasped. "You're kidding."

"It's no joke." The woman sighed again. She smiled. "I'll love all five of them, I know I will. But I'll admit it's not what I expected." She sat up straighter and looked around. "Tony? Marco? Where did they get to?"

Charles heard an explosion of giggles from behind the magazine rack.

The woman shook her head. "It's nonstop," she said. "They are always up to something. If they're not climbing on the furniture, they're mushing Play-Doh into the rug or stuffing toilet paper into the heating vents. My husband says it's like we already have five kids."

Charles was enjoying this conversation, if only because it took his mind off the shots. "Can you tell them apart?" he asked. From what he had seen, the two boys looked exactly alike, except for the color of their overalls: one pair was red and one was green.

"Oh, sure," said Mrs. Cavallo. "Marco, the one in red, has a dimple in his right cheek. Tony has a little scar over his eyebrow from the time he ran into an open drawer in the kitchen. And right now, he's got a very runny nose, as well. I think he caught the cold that Marco had last week. That's why we're here."

"Dr. Lopez is ready for you, Charles," said Martha.

Charles frowned. He did not feel ready for Dr. Lopez. He looked at his mom. "Maybe we should let the twins go first," he said.

"That's a nice thought, Charles," said his mother.

"Oh, that would be such a huge help," said the woman. "We have a long list of errands after this, and I don't know how I'm going to get everything done. Boys!"

There was a rustling sound behind the sofa and two heads popped up. "Let's get our medicine from Dr. Lopez," she said. "Then we can go let Gizmo out of the car."

"Bad Gizmo!" said Marco.

"Naughty Gizmo," said Tony.

"Who's Gizmo?" asked Charles.

Mrs. Cavallo let out one last, long sigh as she struggled to her feet. "Believe it or not, on top of everything else, we also have a puppy."

CHAPTER TWO

"Charles?" Martha, the receptionist, looked at him over her glasses a few minutes later. "Cindy will take you to an examination room now, and Dr. Lopez will be with you in a moment."

Charles was disappointed. He had been hoping to see the twins again. It was so much fun to watch all the mischief they could get into, even in that tiny waiting room. Plus, he'd wanted to find out more about their puppy.

"Let's go," said Mom.

"I can go by myself," said Charles. "I'm not a baby." He remembered when he used to have to sit on his mom's lap while he got shots. He was way too grown-up for that now.

"I want to hear what Dr. Lopez has to say." Mom wasn't taking no for an answer.

The room was chilly, with bright fluorescent lights overhead. Charles shivered as he sat on the end of the high exam table, waiting for Dr. Lopez. *Bang!* He heard a door slam and the patter of footsteps running down the hall. "That must be the twins," he said to his mother.

She nodded and smiled. "That poor mom. She seems a little overwhelmed."

There was a soft knock on their door, and Dr. Lopez came in. "Charles." She smiled at him over her shoulder as she washed her hands at the sink. "I think you've grown at least a foot or two since I saw you last."

Charles couldn't help smiling back. Dr. Lopez really was the nicest doctor ever.

"Let's get this over with," she said. "I know you're not fond of shots, but you wouldn't want to get the flu that's going around, either. Roll up your sleeve."

Charles rolled. Then he turned his head so he wouldn't have to see the needle in her hand. He stared at a gross poster about skin diseases.

"And you're going to be starting basketball, huh?" Dr. Lopez wiped his arm with the cool alcohol.

Charles's nose wrinkled at the smell. "Maybe," he said. "Unless there's something wrong with me."

"You look like a pretty healthy specimen," said Dr. Lopez. "But we'll check you out. Hey, I have a good one for you. Knock-knock."

Charles smiled. Dr. Lopez knew he loved jokes. "Who's there?" he asked.

"Arthur." Dr. Lopez had already started to laugh.

"Arthur who?" Charles asked.

"Arthur any cookies left?" Dr. Lopez cracked herself up.

Charles laughed, too. That *was* a good one. He couldn't wait to tell Sammy and David.

"Okay," said Dr. Lopez. "Let's do that exam."

"What about the shot?" Charles turned to look at her.

"Just did it." She winked at him. "Nothing like a little laughter to keep away the pain." She asked him to pull up his shirt, and then she put a stethoscope to his chest. She listened to his back, too, and made him take deep breaths. She poked into his ears, looked down his throat, and boinged his knee with her little rubber hammer. "All set." She made some notes in his chart, then scribbled something on a small pad of paper and handed it to Mom. "You're as healthy as healthy can be." She squeezed his arm. "Strong, too. I bet you're a fast runner."

"Pretty fast," Charles told her. "I won the hundred-yard dash at our field day."

"Good for you." She stood up and hung her stethoscope back around her neck. "Soon you'll be tearing up the basketball court, too." She smiled at Charles and his mom, and left the room. The whole appointment had taken about five minutes.

"That was quick," said Mom. "And we've got your note for basketball. Ready to head home?"

The second they stepped outside, Charles heard excited barking. He looked toward the parking lot and spotted Mrs. Cavallo and her twins — and the puppy! He was a small pointy-nosed dog, white and brown, with a ruff of fluffy white fur around his neck and a long, fluffy tail. His high-pitched bark echoed among the cars, along with the twins' shrieks. They jumped up and down with their hands in the air as the dog spun around in circles between them. "Quiet, Gizmo!" they yelled. "Stop barking!"

Their mom just stood there, holding the leash and shaking her head. As Charles and his mom got closer, he could see that Mrs. Cavallo looked as if she was about to start crying. When she saw them, she managed a smile. "Meet Gizmo," she called over the barking.

"He's cute," Charles yelled back. "What kind of dog is he?"

"He's a —" Mrs. Cavallo grabbed each twin by the back of his overalls. "Cool it, guys. Time to get ready to go, now that Gizmo's had his walk."

As soon as the boys stopped yelling and jumping around, the dog began to quiet down, too. He came over to sniff Charles's shoes with his sharp little nose.

"He's a sheltie," Mrs. Cavallo said. "A Shetland sheepdog. I've always had shelties. Love the breed — they're so sweet and smart. My last one died just after I got married. Then I waited almost two years after the twins were born, until I felt like we were ready to handle a dog. Gizmo is the greatest — but my timing sure wasn't. I found out I was pregnant again about three weeks after we got him." She gave the boys a gentle push toward the van. "Hop inside now," she said.

"How old is he?" asked Mom. Gizmo was calm enough now that Charles could bend down to pet his long, soft coat. The puppy looked at him with bright, alert eyes and put up a paw for a shake. Charles smiled as he took it. This was one smart dog.

"Only eight months." She sighed. "He's still just a pup, with lots of puppy energy. We've done some basic training with him, but these days I barely have enough time to take him for walks. I'm going to have to find a doggy day care for him. I think

he'll be spending every day there after the triplets arrive."

"Aww." Charles stroked Gizmo's fuzzy ears,
which stood partway up like floppy triangles.
There was nothing wrong with doggy day care. In
fact, Charles's aunt Amanda ran a doggy day care
called Bowser's Backyard, and dogs loved going
there. But it was a shame for a puppy to have to
go every single day. Charles looked up at Mom
with a question in his eyes.

Mom looked thoughtful. "You know," she said.
"It just so happens that our family fosters
puppies. . . ."

"Oh, really?" Mrs. Cavallo looked very interested. "I'd like to hear more about that. I've been
wondering if it might be time to" — she low-
ered her voice so the twins wouldn't hear — "find
Gizmo a home where he'll get the attention he
deserves. Could you — would you —"

Mom held up her hands. "I can't promise that we could take him for the long term," she said. "Not until we talk it over with the rest of the family."

Charles felt his stomach sink. He already liked Gizmo — a lot.

"But how about this?" Mom asked. "We could certainly keep him for the rest of the day, if that would be a help."

Mrs. Cavallo gasped and threw her arms around Mom. "You're a lifesaver!" she said.

CHAPTER THREE

"I normally wouldn't trust my dog to a complete stranger." Mrs. Cavallo spoke over her shoulder as she rummaged through the back of a very messy maroon van. Charles saw takeout food wrappers, library books, bike helmets, rain boots, and lunch boxes all jumbled together. "Now where's that extra leash?" she muttered. "But somehow I trust you. Dr. Lopez said you were a nice family. Not to mention that Gizmo is usually a lot more shy around strangers, but he likes you." She glanced back at Charles.

"I always say Charles speaks Dog," said Mrs. Peterson. "All my kids do, actually. They just seem to know how to make dogs feel comfortable and secure."

Mrs. Cavallo had her head back in the van again. "That's great," she said as she dug through the mess. "I can tell you'll take good care of Gizmo. And it'll be such a help. He just gets so *wired* sometimes, and then the boys get all stirred up, and then my husband worries that he'll nip one of them. Oh, good, here's his favorite toy. I mean Gizmo's, not my husband's —" She handed Charles a stuffed purple turtle, then threw up her hands. "Argh! I can't find it. One leash is enough anyway, right? Because if not —"

Mom put a hand on her arm. "One leash is fine," she said. "We have other leashes at home in case we need another for some reason."

Mrs. Cavallo nodded. "Right. Okay. Thanks. Boys!" She whirled into action, buckling the twins into their car seats and supplying them each with a sippy cup and a handful of Goldfish. "Here's my information." She scribbled some numbers on a crumpled napkin and handed it to Charles's mom. "I can't thank you enough, honestly I can't. I should be home by six, and then maybe my husband can pick Gizmo up, but first I'm off to the pharmacy, and then the grocery store, and then I have to drop off some dry cleaning, and stop by a friend's house to get some hand-me-down clothes, and —"

Mom nodded sympathetically. "Mmmhmm," she murmured. "Go on and do your errands. Gizmo is in good hands."

Finally, Mrs. Cavallo climbed into the driver's seat, started the van, and drove off. The twins waved from their seats. "Bye, Gizmo," they called through the open windows. "Bye!"

Charles and his mom looked at each other. "Whoa," said Charles.

His mom nodded. They both started to laugh. Then his mom shook her head. "I must be nuts, taking this wild little dog even for a day. What was I thinking?"

"But, Mom, maybe he's not really that wild. Look at him now." Charles pointed to Gizmo, who sat waiting patiently next to him. Gizmo looked up at him and wagged his tail.

What's next? I guess you're in charge now.

"Good boy, Gizmo." Charles reached down to pet the puppy's head. "I think it's the twins who get him all excited. Didn't you see how they were jumping around and yelling and waving their hands in the air?"

"True." Mom eyed Gizmo.

"The Bean never does that. He's learned how to act around puppies. But Mrs. Cavallo probably just hasn't had time to teach the twins that it's much better to be calm and quiet and stay still if you want your dog to calm down." Charles looked into Gizmo's bright eyes. "Isn't that right, Gizmo?"

Gizmo sat up on his hind legs, with his paws held up in front, and looked right back into Charles's eyes.

Whatever you say!

Charles laughed. "Look at you, sitting pretty."

"Well, I hope you're right and he's not a total maniac," said Mom. "We'll see how he gets along with Buddy. At any rate, it's nice to be able to do someone a favor. That woman needs all the help she can get."

They walked over to their silver van and Charles opened the door. He was just about to tell Gizmo to "hop in," the way he usually told Buddy, but Gizmo didn't need to be told. He sailed gracefully into the car and settled himself on a seat, all in one quick, easy motion. He faced forward, his ears upright, eyes focused through the windshield.

All set. Where are we going?

"Did you see that?" Charles asked his mom, but she was busy finding her car keys. Charles climbed in next to Gizmo and buckled up. Gizmo leaned against him with a sigh, and Charles petted the dog's long, silky fur. He thought Gizmo seemed relieved to be in the quiet car. "He looks just like a tiny collie, doesn't he?"

Mom raised her eyes to the rearview mirror as she started the van. "He does," she said. "I'm sure Lizzie will be able to tell us lots more about shelties when we get home."

Lizzie was always full of information about dogs and dog breeds. Charles knew she would like Gizmo — but he hoped she would be too busy to spend much time with him. Charles could already tell that Gizmo was going to be lots of fun to play with, and he didn't want his sister hogging the new puppy. Who knew how long they would have him for?

Gizmo sat quietly through the ride home, sometimes watching out the window and sometimes snuffling Charles's hand. "See? I'm a nice guy," Charles told him. He knew that dogs depended on their sense of smell as a way of learning about the world. He hoped that he smelled good to Gizmo, like someone who was kind and trustworthy.

When they pulled into the driveway at home, Gizmo sat up. As soon as Charles unbuckled his seat belt, Gizmo started to climb over him. "Hey, wait," said Charles.

And Gizmo — amazingly — waited. He sat back down on the seat, gazing at Charles with focus. "Wow," said Charles. "Good wait." How many times had they tried to teach Buddy the "wait" command? Lizzie said it would be really helpful, to keep him from bolting out the door or trying to chow down his food before they had put the dish on the floor. Buddy didn't like to wait. But Gizmo seemed to be well trained and to want to please Charles.

Charles made sure that Gizmo's leash was clipped on. Then he reached over to open the door of the van. Gizmo sat as still as a statue, though Charles could see his muscles quivering with the effort. Charles got up and stepped out of the van. "Okay, let's go," he said. Instantly, Gizmo leapt after him.

"Hey!" Lizzie came running out of the house. "Who's this? A sheltie? Are we fostering him? He's adorable."

Gizmo began to spin around in circles, chasing his feathered tail and barking.

Yes, yes, yes! Isn't it wonderful?

"Easy, now," said Mom. "This dog is excitable, to say the least. We need to stay calm around him."

Lizzie dropped to her knees. "Shelties are like that. They're very sensitive to everything that's going on around them. What's his name?"

"Gizmo," said Charles. "He can sit pretty, and wait, and shake hands, and all kinds of things. He's such a smartie. But we might only have him for today."

"Hi, Gizmo." Lizzie scratched between his ears. "Aww, he seems like a real sweetheart. Let's take him and Buddy out in the backyard and see how they get along."

"Great idea," said Mom. "But you're going to have to do it on your own. Charles has another obligation."

Charles turned to stare at his mom. "I do?"

"Don't you remember?" she asked. "I'm driving you and Sammy over to David's. You made a plan with your friends, and you should stick to it. Sammy's counting on us for a ride, and David is expecting you both to come over for basketball practice."

"But . . ." Charles couldn't stand it. Why did Lizzie get to play with Gizmo? What if Mr. Cavallo came to pick him up before Charles even got home? "It's not fair."

"It's not fair to let your friends down, either," Mom said firmly.

Charles knew that tone of voice. It meant "no arguing." He reached down to stroke the pup's soft fur one more time. "Bye, Gizmo." Gizmo leaned against him and looked up at Charles with sad eyes.

What's the matter? Don't worry. I'll be your friend.

"Aww," said Charles. "It's like he knows I'm sad to leave him. It's okay, Gizmo." He did his best to sound cheerful and reassuring. Lizzie was right, as usual. Gizmo was a very sensitive puppy.

CHAPTER FOUR

"This is going to be great," Sammy said as he climbed into the van next to Charles. "Isn't it cool that David's dad put up a hoop at their house? We'll get to play all the time, and . . ."

Charles was hardly listening to his friend's chatter. He sat with his arms across his chest, staring out the window as he replayed the image of Lizzie happily leading Gizmo into the back-yard. Gizmo had pranced along beside her, ready for whatever came next.

"You know," said Mom from the driver's seat, "I have a pretty strong feeling that Gizmo will still be with us by the time Sammy's mom brings you boys home."

"Gizmo?" Sammy asked. "What a great name. Who — or what — is Gizmo?"

"He's a puppy," said Charles.

"Cool. What kind? Are you fostering him?"

"He's a sheltie," said Charles. "You know, the ones that look like miniature collies? So far he's just staying with us for the day, but maybe . . ." He glanced at the back of his mom's head and held up crossed fingers to show Sammy. "He's really cool. He's smart, and he can jump like anything."

Once he started talking about Gizmo, Charles felt a little better. But not a lot better. He still wished he could have stayed home with the new puppy. And not just because he really liked Gizmo. The truth was he was not looking forward at all to shooting baskets with David and Sammy.

The truth was Charles had a secret.

A secret that even his best friends did not know.

Charles had never, ever made a basketball go through the hoop. He hadn't made a foul shot, or a three-pointer, or a layup, or a hook shot. He hadn't swished it, or banked one in, or seen the ball roll around the hoop and then drop through.

Never. None of the above. Not once.

Nobody had noticed, since all the other times he'd played basketball had been in gym, or on the playground, where twenty or thirty other kids milled around throwing basketballs, running up and down, dribbling, and trying to guard one another. Nobody really paid attention to what anybody else was doing.

Charles didn't know what the problem was. He was short, but he was not the shortest boy in second grade. That was Van Stevens. Charles was a little taller than Van and taller than Corey Flant, the second-shortest boy. Charles actually had paid attention during gym class, and he had seen both Van and Corey sink baskets like there was nothing to it.

He knew there was a *lot* to it. It had to do with aim, and timing, and the way you held the ball, and a bunch of other things — things Charles just could not seem to get right.

Because of this problem, Charles had another secret. He knew he was going to look like a jerk when basketball started. It wasn't such a big deal. After all, it was just an after-school program for second graders. It wasn't the NBA, or even the high school team. But Charles still cared. He did not want everyone to laugh at him.

"Sammy's mom will pick you up at five-thirty," Mom said as Charles and Sammy climbed out of the van at David's house. "Have fun, boys."

Charles glanced at the shiny new basketball hoop mounted above the garage door. Its net was bright white, and the orange rim gleamed in the sun. He felt a little flutter of hope in his stomach. Maybe this would be the day that it all finally came together for him. Maybe this would be the day he would finally sink a basket. "Bye, Mom," he said. "Tell Gizmo not to leave before I get back."

Before they could even go up to the door, David came out of the house with a basketball, as shiny and orange and new as the hoop. "Yeah," he said when he saw Charles and Sammy. "Let's play!" He tossed the ball to Charles, and Charles caught it. He smelled that new rubber smell and felt the grippy texture on his fingertips, and he felt hopeful again.

"Shouldn't we warm up a little first?" Charles

asked. "That's what the high school team always does. They run around and practice dribbling and passing and stuff." Charles went to a lot of high school games, because his friend Harry was a big star on the team.

Sammy shrugged. "Sure, why not? Pass it here, Cheese." He held up his hands.

"Okay, Salami," said Charles as he threw the ball. Sammy passed it back to David and they stood in a circle for a while, tossing the ball back and forth. Then they did some dribbling, with each boy taking a turn trying to dribble a figure eight around the other two boys. Charles liked dribbling. He'd practiced dribbling a lot, up and down his driveway, and he had no trouble keeping up a steady rhythm as he wove his way past his friends.

Then, as Sammy finished his second turn of dribbling, he turned toward the basket, ran a few steps, and tossed the ball toward the hoop. "He shoots, he scores!" he cried as the ball bounced off the backboard and fell into the hoop.

David grabbed the rebound and took his own shot, from all the way over by the bushes on the side of the driveway. "A three-pointer!" he yelled as it arced through the air. Sure enough, the ball swished through the net.

"Way to go, Donut!" yelled Sammy.

Charles cheered, too, but he felt jealous. Sammy and David had both been in basketball programs before, and it showed. How would he ever catch up to them?

This time, the ball bounced toward Charles. He reached for it and held it tightly between his hands for a moment as he took a deep breath. Here it came. His very first basket. He took three steps toward the basket, pumped his arms the way the other boys had, and threw the ball in a high arc. *Bang!* It bounced off the backboard and flew back toward him — fast. He barely had time to put his hands up to catch it.

"Tough one, Cheese," said Sammy. "Try again."

Charles looked down at the ball in his hands. Then he shook his head and threw it to David. "Your turn," he said. His heart felt heavy. Nothing was different; nothing had changed. New hoop or not, Charles still could not make a basket.

CHAPTER FIVE

"Let's play H.O.R.S.E.," Sammy suggested after a while.

Charles groaned. He hated that game. They'd played it in gym a few times. The way it worked was that a player took a shot at the basket. If the first player made it, the other players had to make the same shot from the same place on the court. If you didn't make it, you got a letter. First *H*, then *O*, then *R* . . . If you spelled out the whole word "horse," you were out. Charles was always the first one to spell it. Always.

That day was no different. Sammy and David took shots from all over the place — from the end of the driveway, from the bushes, from right below the basket, even once from the side porch. They laughed and high-fived and jumped up and down every time they made a hard shot. And they pretended not to notice when Charles missed shot after shot after shot. Which, Charles thought, made it even worse. After he'd spelled H.O.R.S.E. twice, he was tired of the whole game. "I don't feel so good," he said to David. "Okay if I use your phone to call my mom? Maybe she can pick me up early."

Mom came right away. "What's the matter, honey?" she asked as Charles buckled his seat belt.

Charles muttered something about horse.

"You're feeling hoarse?" Mom asked. "Your voice sounds fine to me. Do you have a fever? I hope we didn't get you that flu shot too late." She reached back to touch Charles's forehead with a cool hand.

"I'm not hoarse," Charles said. "I just stink at basketball."

"Oh, honey." Mom pulled the van out of David's driveway, waving to the two other boys. "Why do you say that? I'm sure you're just as good as Sammy and David."

Charles shook his head. "I stink," he repeated. "I never make any baskets. I'm not going to sign up for basketball after all."

"There's a lot more to basketball than just shooting baskets," Mom said. "I'm sure you're good at running, and passing, and —"

"Nobody cares about that stuff." Charles leaned against the window.

"I have some good news," Mom said. "Maybe this will cheer you up."

Charles slumped further down in his seat. "What?" he asked.

"Aunt Amanda is coming for dinner."

"Oh." Charles liked his aunt, but he saw her all the time. What was so great about her coming over?

Mom smiled at him in the rearview mirror. "She's coming because she wants to meet our new foster puppy."

Charles sat up. "New — wait a minute, are we keeping Gizmo?"

Mom nodded. "Mrs. Cavallo called. She and her husband already talked it over and they decided that it just wasn't fair to keep Gizmo, since they already can't give him the attention he needs. They love him, and it wasn't an easy decision, but they think it's the right one. I promised that we would find him a good home."

The news did cheer Charles up. In fact, he couldn't wait to get home to see Gizmo again. The minute Mom pulled into the driveway, Charles jumped out of the van and ran into the backyard.

Lizzie waved at him as he opened the gate and let himself into the fenced area.

"You won't believe what this dog can do," she said. "He's amazing. Watch this." She clapped her hands. "Here, Gizmo," she called, and the pup bounded toward her. "Up!" She made a motion with her hand, and Gizmo leapt like a feather onto the deck, which was almost the height of Lizzie's waist. "Good boy," she said. Gizmo wagged his tail and nuzzled her face.

"Wow." Charles felt another twinge of jealousy in his stomach, about dogs this time, not basketball. Lizzie was good at dog training, and Gizmo already seemed to like her a lot. "Here, Gizmo," he called, and Gizmo bounded down the stairs and ran right to him. The puppy circled Charles, looking up at him and wagging his fluffy tail. Then he sat up pretty with his paws out in front.

Good to see you again, friend.

Charles laughed. "What a cutie. I think he remembers me." He reached out to scratch Gizmo between the ears. The sheltie pup sat down and gave Charles his paw.

"Of course he does," said Lizzie. "He's a little smartie, isn't he?" She came to pet him, too. Then Buddy galloped over to shove his way into the circle.

"Don't be jealous, Buddy." Charles rubbed his puppy's ears. "We still love you best."

Lizzie and Charles played in the yard for a long time with both dogs. Buddy mostly chased his ball, but Gizmo liked to be challenged. It seemed as if there was nothing he couldn't or wouldn't do. He climbed up the slide on the swing set. He leapt onto the picnic table. He walked along the low stone wall around the rosebushes. Charles and Lizzie were always careful to stay close enough to catch him if he fell or stumbled, but he never did.

Aunt Amanda arrived just in time to see Gizmo jump over a broomstick Lizzie held out for him. "Wow!" she said. "Look at him go." She settled herself on the deck while Lizzie and Charles showed off all the things Gizmo could do. "That's amazing, but remember, he's just a puppy," she said. "He shouldn't be jumping too high or doing anything dangerous. His bones are still growing and his muscles aren't as strong as they will be when he's older."

"I wish there was an agility class around here that he could take," said Lizzie.

Charles knew that Lizzie had been interested in agility — a sport where dogs ran through a sort of obstacle course — for a long time, ever since they had fostered a border collie puppy named Flash. He'd always thought it sounded like fun, too. It would be perfect for Gizmo.

"Funny you should say that," said Aunt Amanda. "There's a woman named Carmen, a dog trainer, who calls me every once in a while to ask if I want her to teach agility classes at Bowser's Backyard. I keep telling her that my hands are full already, but lately I've been thinking it might be time to offer my clients something new. I'll look for her number and give her a call."

Charles knelt down by Gizmo and buried his face in the puppy's fluffy ruff. Who cared about stupid old basketball when you could have so much more fun with a dog?

CHAPTER SIX

"So, who knows what agility is all about?" Carmen asked the very next night. Carmen was small, with curly dark hair and bright eyes. She reminded Charles of a peppy little terrier.

Charles looked down at his sneakers. He suddenly felt shy, even though he'd spoken right up when class had first started and Carmen had asked them to introduce themselves and the dogs they'd be handling. "I'm Charles," he had said then. "And this is Gizmo, a puppy my family is fostering. He's a sheltie and he's really fast and smart." He had looked down with pride at the puppy by his side.

The whole agility thing had happened fast. Aunt Amanda had called shortly after she'd left their house the night before. "It's all arranged," she had told Charles when Mom had handed him the phone. "Carmen is going to give us some classes this week — just you, me, and Lizzie — so I can decide whether I want to hire her to teach a regular class at Bowser's. We start tomorrow night, and I want you to handle Gizmo. Lizzie can bring Buddy, since she has always wanted to try agility with him. And I'm going to see how Lionel likes it." Lionel was one of Aunt Amanda's three pugs.

Now, as they got ready to start their first class, Charles glanced at his sister when Carmen asked her question. He knew Lizzie was wishing she was Gizmo's handler, since he was obviously going to be an incredible agility dog. She stuck out her tongue at him, but then she smiled. "Lizzie knows about agility," he told Carmen.

"Oh?" Carmen turned to Lizzie.

"We've seen some videos, and I've read about it a little," Lizzie said. "It's like an obstacle course for dogs, right? They go up and over and through all those things." She waved a hand at the brightly colored equipment — tunnels and jumps and a blue-and-yellow seesaw — that was set up all around them on the rubber-matted floor of the doggy day care's playroom.

"That's some of what it's about," agreed Carmen. "The dogs have to learn how to do all the obstacles, including a few I haven't brought today. At the higher levels, when dogs are competing, it's about doing the obstacles in a certain order that only the handler knows. The handler has to communicate with the dog about when to do each obstacle."

In the videos, Charles remembered, the handlers ran along next to the dogs, encouraging

47

them and pointing out which piece of equipment to tackle next. It was exciting, especially when they were racing to beat the time of another dog and handler. Any mistakes they made would mean fewer points, so they had to be fast but get everything just right, too.

"So what agility is really all about is the connection between the handler and the dog," Carmen went on. "It's a joyful sport, with lots of positive praise for the dogs."

Charles nodded as if he were listening, but in fact he had started to tune Carmen out. He looked at the jumps and tunnels and then down at Gizmo by his side. He couldn't wait to see what this puppy could do.

But Carmen wasn't quite done. "I'm going to show you how to do each of the obstacles we have here today, but first I just want to mention a few basic rules. The main one is we never punish our dogs if they don't do what we want them to do. We just praise them for trying, and if they succeed, we make a big happy fuss. I like to use the word 'yes!' as my dog goes through a tunnel or over a jump, and toss a treat ahead of him."

"Why don't you just hand him the treat?" asked Lizzie.

"Good question." Carmen gave Lizzie a big smile. "Because we want the dog running forward all the time, looking for the next thing we'll ask him to do. We don't want him to stop suddenly to take a treat from our hand. We need to keep that flow going."

Charles looked down at Gizmo. The pointy-nosed pup gazed back up at him and thumped his fluffy tail on the floor.

When do we get to play?

Charles could tell that Gizmo was as eager to get going as he was.

"Okay, then," said Carmen finally. "Let's all go over to the tunnel. Keep your dogs on their leashes, and don't let them play with each other. They need to focus on you and pay attention to what you're asking them to do."

The tunnel looked like a giant yellow Slinky that could squinch up to be very short and straight, the way it was now, or pull out like an accordion to be long and curvy, like the ones Charles and Lizzie had seen in agility videos. Charles smiled. Gizmo was going to love this.

Charles stepped right up to the tunnel with Gizmo next to him. "Can we go first?" he asked.

"Sure," said Carmen. "If you'll go to the other end and have a treat ready, I'll hold Gizmo at this end and let him go when you call to him.

Remember, say 'yes!' and toss the treat out in front of him as he comes through."

"Okay," said Charles. He handed the leash to Carmen.

"Hello there, Mr. Gizmo." Carmen smiled down at him. "Aren't you a cutie?" She bent down to scratch him between the ears as Charles walked to the other end of the tunnel. Charles could tell that Carmen spoke Dog, too. Gizmo did not seem shy with her at all. "Ready, Charles?" she asked. "Go ahead and call him."

"Gizmo, come!" Charles called through the yellow tube.

At the other end, Gizmo sat up straight and peered around the side of the tunnel to look at Charles.

"This way, Gizmo." Charles poked his head even farther into the tunnel. "You can do it."

Gizmo barked.

"Let's go, Gizmo." Through the tunnel, Charles saw Carmen give Gizmo a little nudge from behind.

"Go, Gizmo," Lizzie chimed in. "Do the tunnel."

But Gizmo didn't race through the tunnel. He jumped up and began to spin around, barking, until Carmen said, "All right, that's enough for this time. Some dogs just don't get the tunnel when they first see it."

Charles couldn't believe it. Gizmo, who would do *anything* in the backyard, wouldn't do this simple little thing. He wanted to ask for one more try, but the others were waiting. He stood up and trudged back to take Gizmo's leash from Carmen. She smiled and patted him on the shoulder, then turned to Aunt Amanda. "How about Lionel?"

Aunt Amanda handed Lionel's leash to Carmen and went to the other end of the tunnel to call him. Carmen let go of the leash, and Lionel galloped through the tunnel. "Yes!" cried Aunt Amanda. She tossed the treat and Lionel snuffled at it, then gobbled it up off the floor as Aunt Amanda grabbed his leash.

Charles stared. Silly little short-legged Lionel could do it, and Gizmo couldn't? This was crazy.

"Nicely done," said Carmen. "Ready, Lizzie?"

Lizzie stepped up. "Sure," she said. She handed Buddy's leash to Carmen, dug a treat out of her pocket, and went to the other end of the tunnel.

"Come on, Buddy," she cried. Carmen dropped the leash. Buddy paused for a moment. "Buddy," called Lizzie again. Buddy put his head around the tunnel to look at Lizzie and took a step as if he were going to run next to the tunnel instead of through it.

Carmen stepped on his leash and gently put Buddy back at the mouth of the tunnel. "Call him once more," she said.

Lizzie knelt down even further so she was practically inside the other end of the tunnel. "Buddy, let's go!" she said. This time, Buddy went through the tunnel. He wasn't exactly going at top speed, thought Charles, but at least he was going. "Yes!" Lizzie cried, tossing a treat for him.

"Wonderful," said Carmen.

Charles hoped she would offer him another turn, but instead she went on to the next obstacle, a jump with a very low bar, about six inches above the floor. "This will be easy," Charles said to Gizmo. He had seen the puppy jump higher than that dozens of times.

But it turned out that Gizmo wouldn't go over the jump, either. He seemed almost afraid of it, even when Charles took him over to sniff it and see that there was nothing to be scared of. "Don't worry," Carmen said. "It takes some dogs a little longer than others. Gizmo is just a young pup, but he has a lot of potential. Once he gets the idea, I bet he'll be a real champ. Every dog learns differently. We just need to be patient."

Charles watched unhappily as Buddy and Lionel leapt and tunneled and jumped, without barking or pausing. But Gizmo? It turned out that Gizmo was no better at agility than Charles was at basketball.

CHAPTER SEVEN

"Of course you'll do it now," Charles said to Gizmo the next afternoon. In the backyard, with no other people or dogs around, Gizmo was a star. He leapt up and down off the deck, danced around the swing set poles, and even went down the slide. And he was having a blast. There was no question in Charles's mind. The fluffy pup's tail waved constantly, and his doggy grin could not have been wider.

"If only I could shoot baskets that well when nobody was looking," Charles said to Gizmo as they lay under the apple tree, taking a break. He was already dreading that day's practice session at David's. Gizmo panted and licked Charles's cheek.

It's all about having fun.

"Charles," Mom called from the back door. "Someone's here for you."

"For me?" Charles asked. It couldn't be Sammy: he was going straight to David's from a dentist appointment. Curious, Charles headed inside with Gizmo right at his heels.

"Harry!" Charles was surprised to see his tall teenage friend in the kitchen, talking to Mom.

"Hey, man." Harry gave Charles a fist bump. "How's it going?" He smiled down at Gizmo and bent to ruffle his fur. "Cute pup. You guys fostering him?"

Charles nodded. "His name's Gizmo." He squinted up at Harry. "Um, what are you doing here, anyway?"

Harry laughed. "I ran into your mom downtown. She said —" He stopped for a moment, then started again. "I just thought you might want to shoot some hoops together. Over at my house, you know? What do you think?"

Charles glanced at his mom. She must have told Harry how much he stunk at basketball. Should he be mad at her? He wasn't sure. "But what about Gizmo?" he asked her.

"I'll watch him for a little while, and Lizzie can take over when she gets home from walking dogs." Mom smiled at him. "It's fine. Go on with Harry."

He turned back to Harry and shrugged. "Okay, I guess," he said.

Harry's rusty old red sports car was parked out front. The entire tiny backseat was taken up by a dog: Zeke, Harry's huge happy-go-lucky chocolate Lab, who always wore a red bandana. Charles climbed into the front and let Zeke drool an enthusiastic hello all over him while he buckled his seat belt.

Charles loved to ride in Harry's car. It was the only convertible he had ever been in. The wind made it hard to talk, and sometimes Charles got cold. Still, he loved the feeling of riding in the open air, like an important person in a parade. People smiled and waved when Harry drove by. Everybody knew Harry.

All too soon, they pulled up in front of a tidy brick house. "My dad put up this hoop when I was about your age," Harry said as he led Charles around back to a paved basketball court that took up a good part of the small backyard. "Then we kept improving on it over the years. It's my favorite practice spot. I've spent thousands of hours out here, all by myself mostly, working on my skills."

Charles was surprised that a star athlete like Harry would have to practice so much. That couldn't be true. Harry was probably just trying to make him feel comfortable.

"Let's do some passing and dribbling first, okay?" asked Harry. He taught Charles a cool drill where they dribbled up and down the court and passed the ball back and forth in rhythm. "Nice," said Harry after a while. "You've got good hands, and a great feel for the ball."

Now Charles was sure. Harry was definitely just trying to make him feel good. "But I'm a lousy shooter," he said.

Harry shrugged. "That just takes practice. Everybody thinks basketball is all about making baskets, but there's a lot more to it than that." He grinned at Charles. "Still, I can understand wanting to be a good shooter. It's a great feeling when that ball drops in."

He tossed the ball to Charles. "Go ahead. Let's see your best shot."

Charles groaned, but he obeyed. He held up the ball, took aim, and let it fly. The ball soared over the backboard and slammed against the garage wall. Charles groaned again. "See?" he asked when Harry had retrieved the ball.

"Watch how I do it," said Harry. "I'll set myself up right here." He stepped to a spot a little farther away from the basket. "Then I look up at the basket. Bend my knees, pump my arms, take aim at a spot on the backboard, and —" He lofted the ball gently toward the basket. It bounced off the backboard and dropped through with a *swish*. He grabbed the rebound and tossed the ball to Charles. "Try again."

Charles tried again. And again. And again.

Harry was so patient. He grabbed each rebound and tossed the ball back to Charles, along with a comment or a piece of advice. "Don't hold the ball so tightly," he said. "Use a light grip." Or "Remember to bend your knees. You want to get your whole body into it." He shouted encouragement — "Close!" — when the ball banged off the backboard, and moaned sympathetically — "You were robbed!" — when it rolled around the rim and fell out instead of in.

Charles's arms ached, and so did his head. When would Harry realize that this was a total waste of time? He was never going to —

And then he did.

He let go of the ball and it soared in a perfect arc. It bounced off the backboard and dropped neatly through the basket with the same *swish* Harry's ball had made. He stood for a moment, stunned, until Harry grabbed the ball and turned to grin at him. "Yes!" Charles yelled then, pumping a fist in the air.

"Yes," said Harry. "Now you've got it. Did you feel how everything came together when you really focused on what you were doing?"

"I felt it, I felt it," Charles said. "Let me try again." Harry threw him the ball. Charles dribbled it around a little, then stopped, bent his knees, pumped his arms, and aimed. Yes! This was incredible. Charles shot basket after basket. He missed a lot, too — but that didn't matter anymore. Not now, when he knew that he really could do it.

The day got even better when Harry drove Charles over to David's. He felt like a superstar when they pulled up in the red car. David and Sammy stared enviously as Charles got out. Charles sauntered over to them, trying to hide his grin. "Hey, you guys," he said. "Want to play H.O.R.S.E.?"

CHAPTER EIGHT

All through the next day, Charles could not stop smiling. He could shoot! He had scored in front of Harry. He had scored in front of his friends. He was on top of the world. "And I have a feeling you'll do great tonight, too," he said to Gizmo that evening as they walked through the door of Bowser's Backyard. Carmen had suggested that they bring one of Gizmo's favorite toys, since some dogs were more interested in toys than food. Charles patted his jacket to feel for the purple stuffed turtle Mrs. Cavallo had given him. "Maybe Carmen is right. Maybe Mr. Turtle will motivate you."

Aunt Amanda had picked up Charles and Lizzie that night. "I think Carmen knows what she's doing," she said as they walked inside. "She seems to have a lot of experience. I can tell already that this class would be a great addition to Bowser's Backyard."

Carmen was waiting inside the play area — with a dog that looked just like an older Gizmo! "Hi, everyone. This is my dog, Lad," Carmen said. "I had a feeling he'd get along well with all the other dogs, and Amanda said it would be okay to bring him. He knows all the obstacles, so he can help me demonstrate. Some dogs learn best by watching another dog."

Gizmo and Buddy pulled Charles and Lizzie across the room. "He's also a sheltie," Charles said as he watched the dogs touch noses, tails wagging. "Isn't he?"

Carmen nodded. "Lad's a sheltie mix, actually. I

think there's some terrier in there, too. He's been doing agility for three years now. He enjoys it, but I don't think I'll ever compete in official trials with him. He just doesn't have that kind of drive." She clucked her tongue to get Lad's attention. "Okay, enough socializing, pups. Let's get down to business."

But Gizmo did not want to get down to business. He stuck out his paws and put his butt in the air. He wagged his tail as he grinned a doggy grin at Lad.

Come on, let's play!

"Gizmo," Charles said. "Come on." He pulled gently on Gizmo's leash. Gizmo pulled back. He barked. He jumped up and spun in circles, as if he was showing off for the other dog.

"Try to get his attention," Carmen said over the barking. "Take him to a quiet corner and get him to focus on you."

"He likes Lad," Charles said.

"I can see that." Carmen smiled at him. "Lad likes Gizmo, too. Who wouldn't? He's a sweetheart. I'm glad he gets along with other dogs. But he does need to learn to pay attention to you, even with everything else that's going on. Did you bring his favorite toy?"

Charles nodded. He clucked his tongue the way Carmen had, and waved the turtle at the puppy. "Come on, Gizmo," he said. "Let's go." He trotted away from Lad, and Gizmo came along with him. "Good boy," Charles said as he let Gizmo tug at the toy.

"Let's work on the balance board today," said Carmen. "This helps get the dogs ready for the seesaw obstacle, where they have to walk up one end of a seesaw, balance at the center, then walk down the other end."

She showed them the balance board. It was like a very low, very wide red seesaw with one end just a few inches above the floor. Carmen led Lad onto the lower end, praising him for every step he took. When Lad moved past the middle of the board, it tilted and the higher end banged down onto the floor. Lad didn't even flinch. He just walked right off the board. "Yes!" said Carmen as she tossed a treat for her dog.

Gizmo let Mr. Turtle fall out of his mouth. He tugged on the leash. "You want to try it?" Charles asked. "Great, let's go." Charles thought this obstacle looked like it would be as easy as pie for Gizmo. He and the fluffy pup approached the balance board. Gizmo put one paw on the low end. "Good dog," said Charles.

"Yes!" said Carmen and Aunt Amanda.

"You go, Gizmo!" said Lizzie.

Everybody was rooting for Gizmo.

Gizmo took his paw off the board and looked up at Charles.

Do I get a treat now?

"Try again." Charles nudged Gizmo toward the board. "Keep going. I know you can do it."

Gizmo put one front paw on the board. Then the other. Then he hopped back off and began to drag Charles to where Carmen and Lad stood.

Charles sighed. "He doesn't like that obstacle, either," he said. He took Gizmo back to the quiet corner to play with Mr. Turtle as Lizzie brought Buddy to the balance board. He watched Buddy walk right over it as if he'd been doing it every day. "Yes!" said Lizzie, beaming.

Then it was Lionel's turn. Charles found himself hoping that the pug would refuse to go across the board. He did not like being the only one whose dog would not do what he wanted him to do. But Lionel jumped right onto the board and scampered across it, not even seeming to notice when it banged down on the floor. "Yes." Aunt Amanda scooped him up for a big hug after he had gobbled the treat she had thrown for him. "What a good puggle-wuggle."

"Want to try again?" Carmen asked Charles.

He shook his head. "That's okay. Maybe one of the jumps would be better."

It wasn't. Well, maybe it was a little better. At least Gizmo tried to go over the jump this time, when Charles went over it with him. But then Charles's foot hit the crossbar, a piece of plastic pipe, and it clattered onto the floor. Gizmo leapt away.

Yikes! What was that? I'm not going near that thing again.

Charles pleaded. He held out treats. But no matter what he did, he could not convince Gizmo to try the jump again. Finally, he took the puppy back to the quiet corner. He hated to force Gizmo to do anything he didn't want to do. Maybe it would be better if they just gave up on agility.

Meanwhile, Lizzie and Aunt Amanda were having a blast. Buddy and Lionel didn't seem to have any trouble at all with the jump, or with any of the other obstacles. "Yes! Yes!" they kept shouting, until Charles wanted to cover his ears. The worst part was the way they pretended not to notice how terrible Gizmo was at agility, the same way Sammy and David had pretended not to notice when Charles couldn't sink a basket.

At least Carmen didn't pretend. She gave Lad to Aunt Amanda to hold and came to talk to Charles. "I still think Gizmo has lots of potential," she said. "How about if you bring him a little early for tomorrow's class? I can give him my full attention, and we'll figure out how to make agility fun for him." She petted Gizmo's head. "What do you say, Mr. Gizmo?"

Gizmo wagged his tail. Then he sat pretty with his paws up.

Yes, please. Whatever you're asking, that's my answer.

How could Charles say no after that? Later he watched Carmen and Lad work together. They seemed like a good team. Carmen sure did know a lot about training dogs, and she obviously liked shelties. "How would you like to go live with

Carmen and Lad?" Charles asked Gizmo. The puppy, who had been watching also, grinned a doggy grin and wagged his tail.

I like that dog!

"There's only one problem," said Charles. "I think Carmen wants to compete in agility, and she already has one dog who can't do that with her. She probably doesn't need two."

CHAPTER NINE

Charles was disappointed by how badly Gizmo had done again at agility class, but he was still in a good mood. At least he knew he was not going to embarrass himself at basketball. The first practice was after school the next day. When Charles trooped into the school gym along with Sammy and David, he felt ready for anything.

Still, he was surprised to see Harry standing under a basket next to Coach Ridley. "What are you doing here?" he demanded.

"Great to see you, too." Harry grinned at him.

"I mean, I didn't know you were coming," Charles said.

Harry shrugged. "I didn't, either. Coach got so many sign-ups that he decided he needed an assistant. He called me last night. I had such a good time working with you the other day that it was a no-brainer to say yes."

Charles smiled. Now basketball would be even better.

"Charles Peterson, right?" Coach made a check mark on the clipboard he held. "Good to have you. Grab a ball and start warming up."

Charles, Sammy, and David joined all the other kids on the court. Soon the gym echoed with the sound of bouncing balls and excited talk and laughter. Charles ran up and down the court with his friends, trying not to bump into anyone or get in the way of a pass.

After a few minutes of total chaos, Coach Ridley blew his whistle. Charles and some of the other kids stopped in place, but a few kept bouncing balls or tossing them back and forth. Coach blew his whistle again, louder this time. "First rule," he said when everyone was finally quiet. "When the whistle blows, I get your complete attention." He smiled around at the gym full of kids. "I'm glad to have you all here," he said. "We may have enough kiddos for a few teams, so we can play some games — eventually. But our first goal is to teach you the basics."

He pulled Harry forward. "Most of you probably already know who this guy is, if you've ever come to a high school basketball game. Or baseball. Or soccer. Harry does it all, and he does it well."

Harry looked down modestly at his sneakers. Then he smiled and winked at Charles. "Good to be here," he said. "Let's have some fun."

"Harry, why don't you take all the kiddos on this side of the gym" — Coach Ridley swept an arm — "and I'll take the others. We'll start with some passing and dribbling practice."

Charles watched as David and Sammy — who had ended up on Harry's side — went to Harry. He wanted to run to join them, but he knew he should follow Coach Ridley's directions. He stayed put and listened while the coach explained the drill. Soon the gym was full of noise again as both groups started to practice.

"That's it, that's it," said Coach as he ran along next to a girl who was dribbling in a crooked line up the court. "Now pass to Ethan — oops. That's okay. You did fine. Go to the back of the line and you'll have another turn soon."

Coach Ridley seems like a nice guy, thought Charles as he waited his turn. He watched Harry, on the other side, showing Sammy how to dribble with his left hand.

"Okay, Peterson, bring the ball up this way," said Coach. "Nice, nice. Great footwork. Go ahead and pass and — beautiful!" He clapped his hands.

Charles thought of agility class, where they praised their dogs for every little thing they did right. Coach was basically doing the same thing. He encouraged everybody and never said anything negative or mean. Maybe, if Gizmo was a failure at agility and Carmen didn't want him, Coach would like to adopt him. Charles could picture Gizmo and Coach together.

Everyone dribbled and passed for a long time, and then Coach Ridley gave them a five-minute break. "Okay, let's do some shooting," he said when the break was over.

Charles rubbed his hands together. This was what he had been waiting for. He couldn't wait to show off what he had learned to do. He went straight to the head of the line. He caught the ball

Coach tossed to him. He bent his knees and looked up at the hoop to take aim. He pumped his arms. Then he let the ball fly.

"Nice try," said Coach a second later. "Next time, give it a little more oomph. You're just about there."

Charles could hardly believe it. The ball had banged off the corner of the backboard and soared through the air, landing near the bleachers and bouncing beneath them. How could this have happened? He wanted to shout, "I can do it, you know. I really can make shots!" He didn't even want to look around to see if anyone was laughing at him. This was exactly what he had been afraid of in the beginning. How embarrassing.

Charles walked to the end of the line — then kept on walking, right out of the gym.

"Charles, wait." He heard Harry calling him, but he didn't stop. He walked into the empty auditorium, across from the gym doors, and plopped down in a seat in the back row.

Charles stared at the sea of empty seats in front of him. Why had he ever thought he could do well at basketball? It had probably been just some weird coincidence that he had made some baskets over at Harry's and a few more at David's.

Now Coach Ridley — and everybody else in that gym — knew the truth.

Charles stunk at basketball.

"C'mon, dude, what are you doing?" Harry slipped into the seat next to Charles.

"Quitting, that's what." Charles crossed his arms.

"Just because you missed that shot? Forget it. You were distracted. There's a lot going on in that gym, and it's hard to focus. You'll do great once you've had some more practice. Anyway, remember what I told you: it's not just shooting that matters. Believe me, not too many balls are going into baskets in there." He tilted his head toward the gym.

"Sure." Charles crossed his arms tighter.

"Want to know what Coach Ridley said to me during our break?" Harry asked.

Charles shrugged.

"He said, 'Boy, that Peterson kid has good hands. And he listens well, too. He'll be a real team player, I can tell.' That's what he said." Harry leaned forward so Charles couldn't avoid looking at him. "I'm not kidding. That's what he said."

"Whatever." Charles stared down at his lap. So what? He had potential, just like Gizmo. Big deal. So far, they were both failures.

"Look, the whole point of this program is for you to learn how to play. Nobody expects superstars on the very first day," Harry said. "We're all going to learn together. C'mon, don't quit." He nudged Charles's shoulder.

Charles sighed. "Okay," he said. "Fine."

Harry grinned at him. "That will make Coach Ridley very happy," he said. "Now let's go back in there and finish up practice. Next week we get uniforms."

Charles trudged back into the gym and joined the line of kids waiting to try for a basket. This time, when his turn came, he did his best to tune out all the noise and activity in the gym. He imagined himself in Harry's backyard, where nobody was watching. He bent his knees. He kept his touch light. He aimed at a spot on the backboard, and he let the ball sail through the air.

"Yes!" yelled Coach Ridley.

CHAPTER TEN

During basketball practice, Charles had plenty of time to think while he waited his turn to shoot. He had started to wonder why Gizmo had not done well at agility class. Could it be for the same reason that Charles had missed that first basket in the gym?

Maybe Gizmo was too distracted by the new place, the new smells, the strange equipment, the new people, and the new dogs. Maybe the smart little pup needed a chance to focus without all the distractions. Maybe then he'd do better, just as Charles had. Charles hadn't made every basket he'd tried for that afternoon, but he'd sunk a few.

* * *

Carmen was just setting up the tunnel when Charles walked into the play area that night. "Charles!" she said. "Good to see you. And you, too, Mr. Gizmo." She squatted down to pet the fluffy pup. "What a good boy." She looked up at Charles. "Thanks for coming early. I was a little afraid you might not come at all after last time," she said.

"I almost didn't want to," said Charles. "But I think I might have an idea. Could we try Gizmo on the tunnel again, before you set up any more equipment, and before anybody else gets here?" He explained about his own troubles with basketball.

Carmen nodded thoughtfully. "Good thinking," she said. "Shelties are so sensitive to everything around them. He might have just been distracted those other times. It probably was not a good idea on my part to bring Lad to class last time, but I wanted to — well, anyway, it was a good lesson for me."

Charles gave Gizmo's leash to Carmen, then bent down to pet him. It was quiet in the play area. No people yelling 'yes!' No balance board banging onto the floor. No snuffles from Lionel, or happy barks from Buddy, or play invitations from Lad. "Are you ready?" Charles asked. Gizmo looked straight into his eyes.

I'm ready.

Charles went to the other end of the tunnel. He knelt down and called, "Gizmo, this way!" And Gizmo flew through the tunnel as if he'd been doing it all his life.

"Yes!" said Charles as he saw Gizmo's head pop out of the tunnel. He was so excited that he forgot to toss the treat in his hand. Instead, he knelt down and opened his arms wide. Gizmo jumped onto Charles, knocking him backward, and they rolled around on the floor together for a moment. Charles couldn't stop laughing as Gizmo licked his face all over.

I did it! I did it! I can tell I made you happy.

Carmen laughed, too. "I knew he had it in him," she said. "Terrific work, Charles. You were absolutely right. Gizmo just needed to focus."

After they praised and petted him, they tried it again. Gizmo ran through the tunnel over and over, even when Carmen made it longer and made it curve. He ran to Charles, then ran back through the tunnel to Carmen when she called him. "He's a star!" she said. "Let's set up a jump and see how he does."

By the time Lizzie and Aunt Amanda joined them, Gizmo was even doing the balance board. He started at one end and kept on going until — *bang!* — the other end smacked down on the floor and he walked right off it. "Yes," said Charles, as he tossed a treat to Gizmo.

"Look at that," said Aunt Amanda. "I always knew he had potential."

"So did I," said Carmen. She folded her arms and cocked her head at Charles. "But even if he never went through any tunnels, I made up my mind to adopt Gizmo the minute I heard you were fostering him."

"What?" Charles couldn't believe what he was hearing.

"I love shelties," Carmen said, "and he's an extra-special guy. I think he'll be an amazing agility dog, and Lad could use a doggy pal. That's partly why I brought Lad the other night, to see if they would get along. Is Gizmo still available?"

Charles stared at her. He tightened his fist around Gizmo's leash. Gizmo leaned into his leg and looked up at him.

Are you okay? Why did everything get so serious all of a sudden?

Charles tried to smile down at Gizmo. "It's okay, boy," he said. But was it? Was he really ready to give this sweet dog up?

Lizzie nudged him. "Say yes," she hissed.

Charles gulped. Of course he had to say yes. Fostering puppies always meant that you had to give them up when the right owner came along. And Gizmo could not do any better than Carmen. He would get to live with a professional dog trainer and spend his days leaping and running and tunneling.

Still, it wasn't easy to let go. Charles had started to feel a very special bond with this puppy, after all they'd both been through. He looked down at Gizmo. "What do you say, boy?" he asked. Gizmo sat up pretty and gave three short, sharp barks.

"I think that means 'yes.'" Charles bent down to give Gizmo one last hug, then walked him to Carmen and handed her his leash.

Carmen smiled. "Thank you, Charles." She looked into his eyes. "I know Gizmo will never forget you. I hope you'll come see us at our very first agility trial."

"I promise," said Charles. "And maybe you'll come watch me play basketball sometime, too."

PUPPY TIPS

Some dogs love to run and jump and play. Other dogs only like to jump up onto the couch — for a nap! It's good to pay attention to what your dog likes to do, and make time for activities that keep him happy. Don't force him to do things he's afraid of or doesn't like to do. Your dog should trust you to do what's best for him.

Activities like agility, tracking, Frisbee, and flyball — or even games you play in your backyard, like fetch, hide-and-seek, and chase — are all great for your dog. They will help keep him from being bored. (Boredom is the main reason for a lot of behavioral problems.) They will help keep him fit. And best of all, they will help create a wonderful bond between you and your dog.

Dear Reader,

Part of the inspiration for this book was an agility class I took with my new puppy, Zipper. (You can learn more about him on my website, www.ellenmiles.net.) Just like Gizmo, Zipper is a very agile dog in the yard and in the woods. He can jump over a fallen tree, perch on a giant rock, walk along stone walls, and run faster than any dog I've ever known. But when I took him to a beginner agility class, he did not do well at all! He was terrified by most of the equipment and distracted by the other dogs and people. My teacher (her name is Carmen!) was very patient. She helped me try different ways for Zipper to learn, and by the end of our classes, he had gained a lot of self-confidence and was doing much, much better. I look forward to our next set of agility classes with Carmen!

Yours from the Puppy Place,
Ellen Miles

ABOUT THE AUTHOR

Ellen Miles loves dogs, which is why she has a great time writing the Puppy Place books. And guess what? She loves cats, too! (In fact, her very first pet was a beautiful tortoiseshell cat named Jenny.) That's why she came up with the Kitty Corner series. Ellen lives in Vermont and loves to be outdoors every day, walking, biking, skiing, or swimming, depending on the season. She also loves to read, cook, explore her beautiful state, play with dogs, and hang out with friends and family.

Visit Ellen at www.ellenmiles.net.